FROM THE FILMS OF

Harry Potter

CREATE BY STICKER: HOGWARTS

SCHOLASTIC INC.

ISBN 978-1-338-59755-4

10 9 8 7 6 5 4 3 2 1   20 21 22 23 24
Printed in Malaysia   106

First edition 2020

By Cala Spinner
Book design by Jessica Meltzer

REPARO!

Sometimes, things in the **wizarding world** can get a little, er . . .
jumbled. Just ask Seamus Finnigan, who learned during his first
Charms lesson that incanting a spell incorrectly can create an
explosion. Or speak to Hermione Granger, who accidentally
dropped feline hair into her otherwise carefully brewed Polyjuice
Potion. Even Harry Potter—yes, *that* Harry Potter—would admit
that the slightest mispronunciation can land an unsuspecting
wizard in dodgy Knockturn Alley instead of friendly Diagon Alley.
And, as Luna Lovegood would say, sometimes brains can
get a little fuzzy because of a pesky, invisible, and rogue
Wrackspurt floating through a witch or wizard's ears.

In this book, you will find some images that have been,
well, **jumbled** in one way or another. You will need to **repair**
the images by matching the numbered stickers in the back
of the book to the numbers on the **sticker scene**.

When you're done, the image will be complete.
Then you can turn the page and complete the next one,
and the next one, and the next!

IT'S JUST LIKE MAGIC!

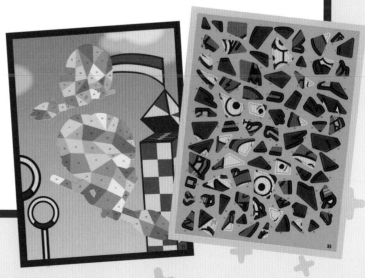

3

Hogwarts School of Witchcraft and Wizardry is the finest school of magic in Great Britain. It is tucked away, located in a secret location in the Scottish Highlands. To get to Hogwarts, witches and wizards board the Hogwarts Express, which leaves from **platform nine and three-quarters** in London.

Use the stickers on page 25 to complete the image of the **Hogwarts Express**!

Harry, Hermione, and Ron met during their first year at **Hogwarts**. They were sorted into Gryffindor house. There are **four houses** at Hogwarts: Gryffindor, Ravenclaw, Hufflepuff, and Slytherin.

Use the stickers on page 27 to create the **school crest**, showing all the houses of Hogwarts!

Hogwarts™

At **Hogwarts**, students learn how to use magic. They take classes in Potions, Defense Against the Dark Arts, Care of Magical Creatures, and Transfiguration, just to name a few!

The headmaster of Hogwarts is **Professor Albus Dumbledore**. Use the stickers on page 29 to create an image of **him**!

DEFENSE AGAINST THE DARK ARTS

Hogwarts is full of **surprises**. Ron learns this in his first year when he must play a large game of wizard chess to help Harry reach the **Sorcerer's Stone**.

Use the stickers on page 31 to **discover** how brave Ron is.

One spell that Harry learns at Hogwarts is called the **Patronus Charm**. The Patronus Charm creates a spirit **guardian** that protects its caster from danger. Harry's Patronus takes the shape of a **stag**!

Use the stickers on page 33 to complete the image of Harry **casting** his Patronus Charm.

Of course, Hogwarts isn't *all* about studies. There's **Quidditch**, too! Quidditch is a wizarding sport that's played on **broomsticks**. In their time at Hogwarts, Harry and Draco were both **Seekers** for their respective house teams.

Use the stickers on page 35 to create an image of Ginny and Harry playing Quidditch for the **Gryffindor team**!

At the end of their third year, Harry and Hermione use a **Time-Turner** to save **Buckbeak** the Hippogriff.

Use the stickers on page 37 to complete the image of their **brave rescue**.

In what would have been her seventh year, Hermione, disguised as **Death Eater** Bellatrix Lestrange, broke into **Gringotts Wizarding Bank** in search of an item necessary to defeat Voldemort. But then the disguise wore off!

Use the stickers on page 39 to find out how Hermione, Harry, and Ron **escape** the bank!

Luna is a true **Ravenclaw**. She's creative and open-minded, and often sees things that others don't.

Use the stickers on page 41 to reveal what Luna can see!

Harry faced many **challenges** during his time at Hogwarts, but one thing kept him grounded: his **friends**.

Use the stickers on page 43 to create an image of Harry, Ron, and Hermione—true friends who are always there for each other, through thick and thin!